The Steadfast Tin Soldier

by

HANS CHRISTIAN ANDERSEN

TRANSLATED BY
M. R. JAMES

Illustrated by MARCIA BROWN

CHARLES SCRIBNER'S SONS *New York*

To HELEN MASTEN
and MARIA CIMINO

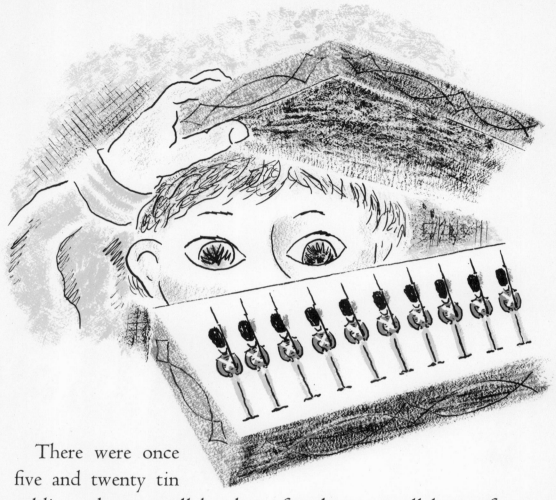

There were once
five and twenty tin
soldiers who were all brothers, for they were all born of
one old tin spoon. They all shouldered arms and stood
eyes front; red and blue was their beautiful uniform.
The very first thing they heard in this world when the
lid was taken off the box they lay in, was the words
"Tin soldiers!" It was a little boy who shouted it, and
clapped his hands: he had been given them because it was

his birthday; and now he set them up on the table. Each soldier was exactly like his neighbour; there was only one who was a little different.

He had one leg. He had been the last to be cast, and there was not enough tin left.

Still, he stood just as steady on his one leg as the rest on their two, and he it is to whom we have to pay attention.

On the table where they were set up stood a great many other toys, but the one which caught the eye most was a lovely paper castle. Through the little windows you could see right into the rooms. In front of it, little trees stood round a tiny looking-glass, which was meant to look like a lake. Swans made of wax swam on it and looked at their reflections. The whole thing was very pretty, but prettiest of all was a little lady who stood in the open door of the castle: she too was cut out of paper, but she had a skirt of the finest possible muslin, and a little painted blue stripe crossing her shoulder like a scarf: in the middle of it was a bright spangle as big as the whole of her face. The little lady had her arms stretched out, for she was a dancer, and one of her legs was lifted so high that the Tin Soldier could not see it, and thought that she had only one leg like him.

"That would be the wife for me," he thought, "but she's very genteel. She lives in a castle, and I have only a box, and there's five and twenty of us to go in it—it's no place for her. Still, I must try to get introduced."

Then he laid himself down at his full length behind a snuff box which was on the table. From there he could look straight at the elegant little lady, who continued to stand on one leg without losing her balance.

In the evening, all the other Tin Soldiers were put into their box, and the people of the house went to bed. Then the toys began to play: they played at paying calls, at fighting battles, and getting up balls. The Tin Soldiers rattled in

their box, for they wanted to join in, but they couldn't get
the lid off. The nutcracker turned head over heels, the slate
pencil made a great to-do on the slate. Such a fuss there
was that the canary woke up and began to talk—in verse, too!

The only two who did not leave their places were the Tin Soldier and the little dancer: she stood stock-still on tip-toe, with her arms spread out; and he was just as steady on his one leg. He did not take his eyes off her for a second.

Then the clock struck twelve, and "crack", up sprang the lid of the snuff box. But there was no snuff in it, no, but a little black troll—it was just a trick.

"Tin Soldier," said the troll, "will you keep your eyes to yourself?"

But the Tin Soldier pretended not to hear.

"All right, wait till to-morrow," said the troll.

Well, when to-morrow came and the children got up, the Tin Soldier was put on the window-sill, and whether it was the troll's doing or the draught, all at once the window flew open and the soldier fell down on his head from the third storey. It was a fearful fall. His leg pointed straight up, and there he stayed on his cap, with his bayonet stuck between two paving-stones.

The nurserymaid and the little boy ran down at once to look for him, but though they as nearly as possible trod on him, they could not see him. If the Tin Soldier had only shouted "Here I am," they would have found him easily enough, but he thought it was not proper to call out loud, seeing he was in uniform.

Next it began to rain. The drops came faster, one after another; it became a regular downpour. When it was over, two street-boys came along.

"Look here," said one of them, "there's a tin soldier. He shall go for a voyage."

So they made a boat out of newspaper, put the Tin Soldier in it, and off he sailed, down the gutter; the two boys ran along with him and clapped their hands. Mercy on us! What billows raged in that gutter, and what a stream was there! There had, indeed, been a torrent of rain. The paper boat tossed up and down and sometimes whirled round and round so that the Tin Soldier became dizzy; but he was as steady as ever, turned not a hair, looked straight in front of him, and kept shouldering arms.

All at once the
boat darted under a
broad culvert. It was as dark there
as if he had been still in his box.

"Where can I be going to now?" thought
he. "Aye, this is the troll's doing. Ah, dear,
if that little lady was here in the boat, it might
be twice as dark for all I cared!" Just then came up
a big water-rat who lived under the culvert.

"Got a pass? Out with your pass!"

But the Tin Soldier said nothing, and held his rifle
tighter than ever. The boat rushed on, and the rat after it.

Ugh! How it gnashed its teeth and called out to the
chips and straws: "Stop him! stop him! he hasn't paid
the toll! he hasn't shown his pass!"

But the stream ran stronger and stronger. Already the
Tin Soldier could see daylight, ahead where the culvert

ended; but at the same time he heard a rushing sound that was enough to appal the bravest heart. Think of it! at the end of the culvert the gutter ran straight into a huge canal. For him it was as dreadful as for us to go down a great waterfall in a boat.

By this time he was so near it that he could not
stop: on went the boat, and the poor Tin Soldier held
himself as stiff as he could—no one should say of him that
he winked an eye.

The boat turned round three or four times, and filled
with water to the gunwale: it was bound to sink.

The Tin Soldier was up to his neck in water.

Deeper and deeper sank the boat.

Softer and softer grew the paper.

The water closed over the Soldier's head, and he thought
of the pretty little dancer whom he should never see again,
and in his ears rang the words:

> "Onward, onward, warrior,
> Death waits for thee!"

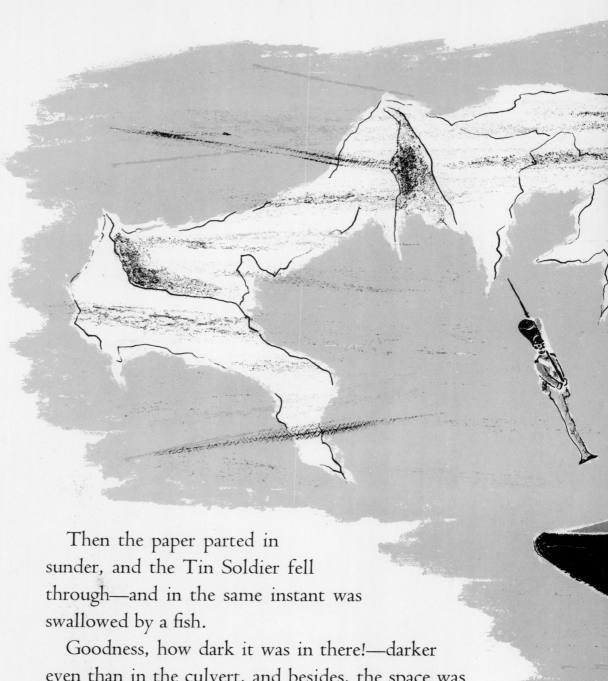

Then the paper parted in
sunder, and the Tin Soldier fell
through—and in the same instant was
swallowed by a fish.

Goodness, how dark it was in there!—darker
even than in the culvert, and besides, the space was
so cramped. But the Tin Soldier was steady as ever
and lay all his length with shouldered arms.

The fish darted hither and thither and executed the most alarming movements. Finally it became quite quiet, then a ray of light seemed to break through. The light shone out full, and somebody called out:

A TIN SOLDIER!

The fact was, the fish had been caught, brought to market, sold and taken into the kitchen where a maid cut it open with a big knife. She took the Soldier by the body in her finger and thumb and carried him into the parlour, where everybody wanted to see the remarkable man who had travelled about in the inside of a fish. But the Tin Soldier was not in the least above himself.

They set him up on the table, and there—well! it is
funny how things do come about in the world—the Tin
Soldier was in the self-same room he had been in before:
he saw the very same children, and the toys were on the
table—the lovely castle with the pretty little dancer, who
was still standing on one leg, with the other lifted
high up. She too was steadfast. The Tin Soldier
was touched, and could have wept tears of tin, but it
would not have been becoming. He looked at her and
she looked at him, but neither of them said a word.

At that moment one of the little
boys picked up the Soldier and threw
him right into the stove. He had
no explanation to give: of
course, it was the troll
in the snuff box who
was responsible.

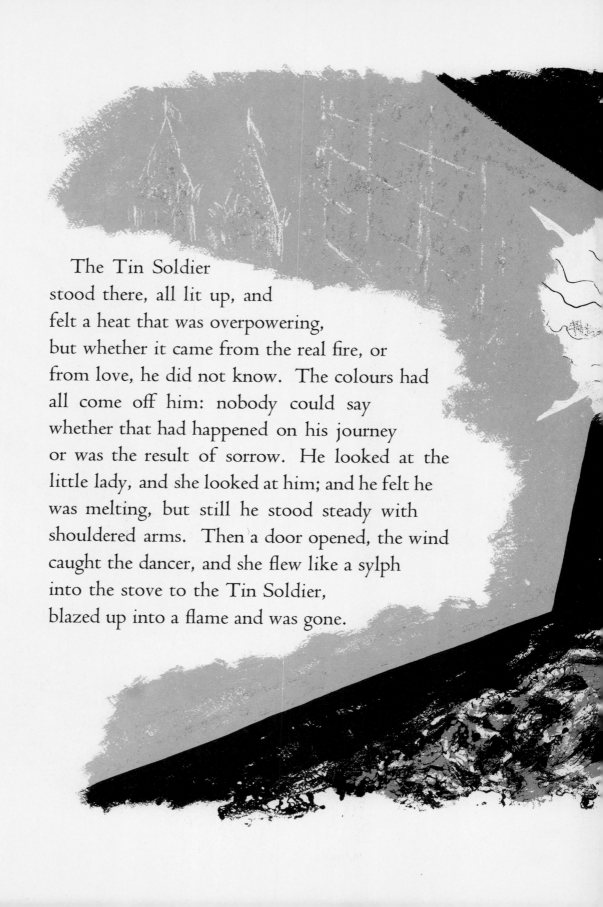

The Tin Soldier
stood there, all lit up, and
felt a heat that was overpowering,
but whether it came from the real fire, or
from love, he did not know. The colours had
all come off him: nobody could say
whether that had happened on his journey
or was the result of sorrow. He looked at the
little lady, and she looked at him; and he felt he
was melting, but still he stood steady with
shouldered arms. Then a door opened, the wind
caught the dancer, and she flew like a sylph
into the stove to the Tin Soldier,
blazed up into a flame and was gone.

The Tin Soldier melted down into a lump, and when next day the maid took out the ashes, she found him in the shape of a little tin heart. Of the dancer, only the spangle was left, and that was burnt as black as a coal.